Clara AND Asha

ERIC ROHMANN

Roaring Brook Press
New Milford, Connecticut

"Clara! Time for bed,"
my mom calls.
But I'm not sleepy,
so I open my window . . .

...and wait for Asha.

We met in the park.

And I brought Asha home.

I showed Asha every room in the house.

My mom said, "Clara, have you gotten into your bath yet?"

I said, "I'm waiting for my turn."

I introduced Asha
to everybody.

On Halloween,
Asha helped me
with my costume.

When it snowed, we
played on the big hill.

And tonight?

Tonight we
play in the sky.

My mom calls,
"Clara, time for bed."

I say, "I'll see you
tomorrow."

"Goodnight, Asha!"

"Go to sleep, Clara,"
my mom says. And I try.
I really, really try, but....

Can I help it if I have
so many friends?

For Candy
and for Simon
who both said, "It's all there in the pictures."

Copyright © 2005 by Eric Rohmann
Published by Roaring Brook Press
Roaring Brook Press is a division of Holtzbrinck Publishing Holdings
Limited Partnership
143 West Street, New Milford, Connecticut 06776

Distributed in Canada by H. B. Fenn and Company Ltd.
Book design by Tania Garcia

Library of Congress Cataloging-in-Publication Data
Rohmann, Eric.
Clara and Asha / Eric Rohmann.—1st ed.
    p. cm.
Summary: Young Clara would rather play with her imaginary giant fish,
Asha, than settle down to sleep.
[1. Imaginary playmates—Fiction. 2. Fishes—Fiction. 3. Bedtime—Fiction.]
I. Title.
PZ7.R6413Cl 2005
[E]—dc22   2005004677

ISBN: 1-59643-031-1

Roaring Brook Press books are available for special promotions and premiums.
For details, contact: Director of Special Markets, Holtzbrinck Publishers.

First Edition August 2005
Printed in the United States of America
10 9 8 7 6 5 4 3 2 1